THE GUMBALL LOTTERY

A DELICIOUS ASSORTMENT OF RHYME

THE GUMBALL LOTTERY
A Delicious Assortment of Rhyme

BY SALLY DOLLAR

ILLUSTRATED BY RORIE SCROGGINS

LUMINARE PRESS

WWW.LUMINAREPRESS.COM

The Gumball Lottery: A Delicious Assortment of Rhyme
© 2019 Sally Dollar

Printed in the United States of America

Cover Illustration: Rorie Scroggins
Cover Design: Melissa K. Thomas

Author Photo: Lisa Little Photography
Illustrator Photo: Max Scroggins

Luminare Press
438 Charnelton St., Suite 101
Eugene, OR 97401
www.luminarepress.com

ISBN: 978-1-64388-051-8
LCCN: 2019933650

For Luke, Anna & Maggie,
who inspire me every day.
—S.D.

For Max & Evie,
who spark my creativity with their
curiosity and adventurous natures.
—R.S.

TABLE OF CONTENTS

IN OTHER WORDS, WHERE YOU SHOULD LOOK TO FIND THE STUFF INSIDE THIS BOOK.

SWEET. FUNNY. INSPIRING. A LITTLE RANDOM...AND A WHOLE LOT OF FUN!

The Gumball Lottery is a delicious assortment of rhyme, brimming to the top with imagination and kid appeal. This collection of 61 poems features memorable characters such as Marco Pollo, an adventure-seeking chicken ("not to be confused with that *other* guy"); a lone "rebel sock" who refuses to settle for the hamper; and a family of pigs who, through trial and error, discover they were always meant to fly.

In the title poem, "The Gumball Lottery," a hopeful kiddo takes a chance in pursuit of a yummy prize. "Dear Mac" features a series of letters between Mac & Cheez, and the final poem, "This is *Not* the End," encourages readers to search for their next adventure. Other rhymes use iconic childhood symbols and experiences as opportunities for lighthearted teaching moments. And other featured rhymes are just. plain. fun.

SO, WHAT ARE YOU WAITING FOR?
GO AHEAD...
TAKE A CHANCE AT *THE GUMBALL LOTTERY!*

FIND YOUR THING

There is a THING that's been given to you.
No, not a bike or a new kazoo.
Though gifts like those would sure be swell,
You've got a THING that you do well.

For example, do you like to write?
Or perform on stage with the lights on bright?
Or is your talent go-kart driving?
It might be deep-sea scuba diving.

Maybe you're a genius at origami
Or making sandwiches from salami.
Do you construct great pillow forts?
There are THINGS of all sorts.

Do you competitive hula hoop?
Or make a delicious noodle soup?
You will see (if your heart is in it),
With your THING, the sky's the limit!

Maybe your knack is basketweaving—
Or being positive and believing.
Do you yodel or collect key chains?
Perhaps you design paper planes.

Remember that THING is yours to find.
It's within your heart and inside your mind.
And once you find it, DO your THING—
Then your mouth will smile and your soul will sing.

DO UNICORNS SAY NEIGH?

Do unicorns say NEIGH?

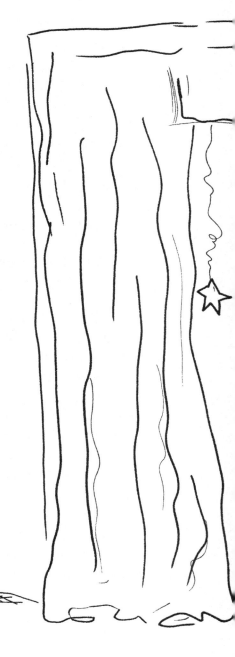

Or do they sing sweet melodies
And talk about tales of old,
Recalling every detail of
The greatest stories ever told?

Do they recite enchanting poems
And hum magical lullabies?
And perform brilliant plays,
Full of wonder and surprise?

Do they give passionate speeches
And invent clever schemes?
Do they whistle in the moonlight,
Living out their wildest dreams?

Or do they just say NEIGH?

SALLY DOLLAR

THE DAY THE PIGS LEARNED HOW TO FLY

One hot and sunny afternoon
On a farm outside of town,
A family of pigs grew tired
Of simply lying around.

"All we do is roll in mud,"
Remarked Mr. Pig.
Mrs. Pig quickly agreed,
"It's time to do something BIG!"

"Then what are we going to do?"
Big Brother Pig chimed in.
"I know—let's learn to fly!"
Little Sis squealed with a grin.

So the pigs got to work
And devised a detailed plan.
They gathered their materials,
And then they all began.

Meanwhile, the chickens looked on
With disbelief and doubt.
"There's no way these crazy pigs
Will figure this one out."

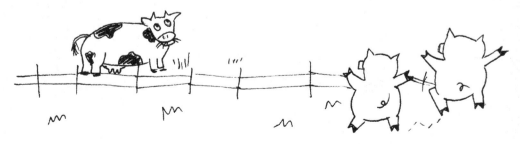

SALLY DOLLAR

As the cows grazed in the grass,
They laughed and joked and sneered.
"Those pigs are pretty kooky.
In fact, they're just plain weird!"

But the pigs kept working day and night
(Despite those that said they were insane).
Then they revealed their masterpiece—
A single-engine plane!

After many hours of practice
(And an accident or two),
The pigs finally figured it out—
And then they actually flew!

Motivated by the pilot pigs
And their act of aerial conquest,
The chickens and cows also resolved
To put something new to the test...

Soon the cows were skydiving;
The hens learned to water ski!
Other critters were inspired, too—
The goats began to bungee!

So on any given sunny day
On the farm outside of town,
Animals can now be seen
Flying and diving and whizzing around.

And the pigs smile and think
Every time they fly again,
"It was never a matter of if.
It was always a matter of *when*."

SALLY DOLLAR

PERSPECTIVE

This morning I had an idea
And asked a pal just what she thought.

She said I should try a new way
To look at this idea I've got.

She said, "You need a fresh perspective—
Try a different view instead."

That's why I decided to think some more
While standing on my head.

WHAT'S
UP?

Dear Mac,

It's really been quite marvelous
Being together all these years,
And I sincerely hope this letter
Doesn't cause too many tears,

But, I just feel like I have
Something very important to say-
I think it's time to take a chance
And each go on our way...

Most Respectfully,
Cheez

P.S. I promise it's not you-it's me.

DEAR CHEEZ,

SAY IT AIN'T SO!

SURE, WE'VE HAD OUR UPS AND DOWNS,
AND SURE, I'VE BEEN BOILING MAD.
BUT YOU ALWAYS SEEM TO BUTTER ME UP,
AND THEN IT'S NOT SO BAD.

AND SURE, SOMETIMES I FEEL BOXED IN,
EVEN SPIRALING OUT OF CONTROL.
BUT YOU ALWAYS SEEM TO COMFORT ME
WHEN WE'RE TOGETHER IN THAT BOWL.

I'M BEGGING YOU TO RECONSIDER.
TAKE ME BACK - PLEASE, PLEASE, PLEASE !
WE GO TOGETHER LIKE MILK AND COOKIES,
LIKE TOAST & JAM - AND WELL, LIKE MAC & CHEESE.

YOUR BUDDY,
MAC

A GIRL NAMED ELLA MINNOW

Let me tell you about my friend—
Her name is Ella Minnow.
Her favorite tune is the alphabet song.
She sings it high; She sings it low.

She sings it everywhere she goes—
All morning, night and in between.
She sings it at school and at home.
She sings it so much, it is routine.

Others ask why she loves the ditty,
Since there's really not much to it.
Although, *I* think it's fairly obvious…
Her name is halfway through it!

SALLY DOLLAR

FRANCINE & HER TAMBOURINE

Francine has a tambourine.
She jingles it everywhere she's seen,
Even on her trampoline—
Francine and her tambourine.

Haley has a ukulele.
She strums it loud while she sings gaily,
And she practices almost daily—
Haley and her ukulele.

Drew has a new kazoo.
He crafted it from old bamboo.
Then he painted it neon blue—
Drew and his new, blue bamboo kazoo.

They form a band one day,
Where they all jingle, strum and play.
It's more fun together anyway.
"We're gonna be famous!" they all say.

And you know what? They just may.

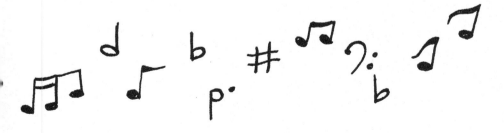

THE GUMBALL LOTTERY   11

ONCE UPON A *HICCUP!*

Listen closely, friends. I'm gonna tell a story.
It's a really, really good one, full of courage, love and glory...

Once upon a time,
In a kingdom by the sea,
There lived a very brave *HICCUP!*
(Oh dear, please excuse me.)

So, as I was saying,
There lived a very brave knight.
He fell in love with a *HICCUP!*
(Gee whiz! It's hard to get this right.)

So, this brave knight fell in love
With a pretty maiden in a castle.
But, at first she didn't *HICCUP!*
(Good golly! This is a hassle!)

SALLY DOLLAR

Anyways, this knight, he loved a maiden,
And at first she didn't love him back,
But then one day he met a *HICCUP!*
(Wow! I'm getting quite off track!)

Okay, the knight met a magic blue fish
While strolling along the beach one day.
The fish granted him one *HICCUP!*
(Oh man! Will these things EVER go away?!)

I'm not sure how long it will take
To finish this tale all the way through,
So, I will just try to *HICCUP!*
I mean…I'll summarize for you…

Brave knight, pretty maiden, castle,
Fell in love, beach stroll, fish of blue,
Got his wish to get the girl,
And they lived happily ever after…*PHEW!*

Well, I guess I finally finished!
I made it to my story's end.
I hope you enjoyed this *HICCUP!*
(Seriously?! Not again!!!)

*If this predicament has ever been yours, please see
the next page for a list of cures.*

THE GUMBALL LOTTERY   13

SO, YOU'VE GOT THE HICCUPS?

So, you've got the hiccups, you say?
Well, let's find a cure right away!

There are plenty of ways you can try
To get those things to go bye-bye.

First, take a drink of H20.
Then hold your breath for a minute or so.

Next, put some sugar in your mouth.
Then stand on your head—point your noggin south.

Or find a friend to give you a scare…
BOO! (Did that work? Are they still there?)

Spin in a circle as long as you please
While counting to thirty-three in Chinese.

What?

Not so sure about that last one I said?
Well, do *you* have any ideas instead?

SALLY DOLLAR

MR. E

I met a curious fella—
His name is Mr. E.
I'm trying to figure him out.
Where's he from, and who is he?

I know very little about him.
He's quite puzzling to me—
The secretive, strange, perplexing,
Mysterious Mr. E.

THE HUG THAT LASTS FOREVER

I have a special present for you;
It's basically the Best. Gift. Ever.
And guess what?! This present's free—
It's a hug that lasts forever.

First, I'll wrap my arms around you,
Then I hope that you will know
That the love in this embrace
Is yours to take wherever you go.

I hope you feel it when you're awake
And when you're fast asleep.
I hope you feel it sitting down
Or when you're standing on your feet.

I hope you feel it every day
While you're going to and fro,
When you're up or down or in-between,
Whether you're high or low.

And when you feel the timing's right,
I hope you give it to a friend.
Then they, too, can pass it on—
This is a hug that has no end.

SALLY DOLLAR

THE STRANGER

A stranger has entered my presence—
Clothed in darkness, so mysterious.
He's following my every step;
This really is quite serious.

A stranger has entered my presence.
I'm not sure what I should do!
He seems taller every minute
While he mimics my every move.

Wait just a second…I KNOW this guy!
There's no need to fear or fret.
I remember now…It's my *shadow*!
(Sometimes I tend to forget.)

THE GUMBALL LOTTERY

Oh, look! A gumball machine!
And I happen to have lots of cents.
It's filled to the top with chewy delights
Just waiting to be dispensed.

Oh, look! I see a PINK one!
Smack in the center of all of those treats.
That one looks the yummiest
Of all of those colorful sweets.

I bet it tastes like strawberry—
How delicious that gumball will be!
And even though I've chosen it,
I like to think that *it's* chosen *me*.

Twist goes the knob…My prize begins
Its descent through the small corridor.
Sliding down 'til its journey ends—
A grand reveal at the tiny door.

Oh, look…I got a BLUE one…
This is *not* the one I picked out.
Guess I'll try again, so I anxiously wait
As another glides down its route.

Now it's GREEN?! But I want PINK!
I'm getting tired of this gumball game.
It's not unfolding like I planned,
But I guess there's no one to blame.

SALLY DOLLAR

Okay, one more time…Now it's RED!
Seriously?! Is this a joke?!
If I keep spending all of my money,
I might just go flat broke.

But…

Maybe there *is* an upside—
I shouldn't feel all that crummy.
At least I've got a handful of gum
That probably tastes just as yummy.

I guess in this game of hope and chance,
There's a lesson to be had—
When you don't get what you want
Sometimes it's not so bad.

In fact, sometimes it's even better.

THE LEGEND OF MARCO POLLO

When you think about world explorers,
It's a pretty impressive list.
Well, there's one trailblazing pioneer
That your history book might have missed.

His name was Marco Pollo*
(Not to be confused with that *other* guy**).
Blessed with a rebellious spirit,
Logic and reason he chose to defy.

SALLY DOLLAR

One day on the farm he flew the coop,
And thrills he decided to seek.
He loved adventure—and just happened to have
Some feathers, eight toes and a beak.

Now, there were some who said to Marco,
"You can't do this. You're *insane*."
But he set forth without fear—
With all of his heart and all of his brain.

With a telescope under one wing,
And an unfinished map in the other,
He traveled the world by foot and by sea,
Finding one new land after another.

He was gutsy and gritty and daring;
He showed confidence with every cluck!
And with each treasure and fortune he gained,
Marco knew it took more than just luck.

His discoveries required courage,
Dedication and moxie, too.
And now the legend of Marco Pollo
Has made its way to YOU.

So next time you're studying history
In your class at school,
Or when you're playing water games
With your buddies at the pool…

Remember Marco's legacy
And how he was bold and brave.
(And if someone ever calls YOU "chicken,"
It's actually a compliment they gave.)

*Pollo (poy-oh): Spanish for "chicken." Technically, in most Span-
ish-speaking cultures, "cooked chicken." Rest assured, however,
the hero of our story lived a long and productive life. Marco never
ended up on anyone's plate—rather, he ended up a legend.

**That "other guy": Marco Polo (one "l," not two!) was a famous
Italian adventurer who explored Asia and wrote about his journeys.
No, he did not have feathers, eight toes and a beak.

SALLY DOLLAR

TO MRS. MURPHEY

To Mrs. Murphey (my favorite teacher):

I just wanted to let you know—
I don't have my homework today.
But there's a very good explanation
That's quite convincing, I must say.

It's actually a funny story—
There's no need to fret or fuss.
Well, my dog Spot—he ate it.
I'm telling the truth, I promise!

Then guess what happened next?!
(Which further proves it's not my fault.)
Spot smacked his lips, smiled and said,
"I think this needs some more salt."

Can you believe it?!

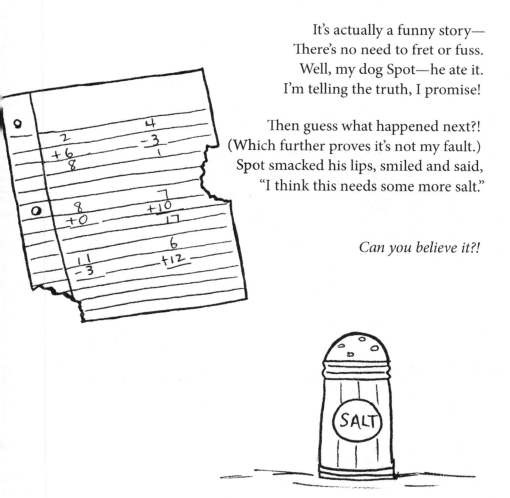

THE HOUSE

In a far-off place on the edge of town
There's a house where books and love abound.
And a family lives inside this home
Where joy and trees and flowers have grown.

They sing and dance and read and play
And laugh and hug and hope and pray.
They think up dreams of every sort,
While the days are long, but years are short.

They try their best to live in light
And thank the Lord and kiss goodnight.
Yes, there's lots of promise to be found
In the house where books and love abound.

SALLY DOLLAR

THE PATH

One day I started down a path,

Not sure what I would find.

But I kept on going anyway,

Because this path was mine.

There were hills and peaks and valleys—

Surprises often came.

But I kept on pressing forward,

In and out of sun and rain.

Although the path was winding,

With lots of turns along the way,

It led me right where I belong—

It led me to today.

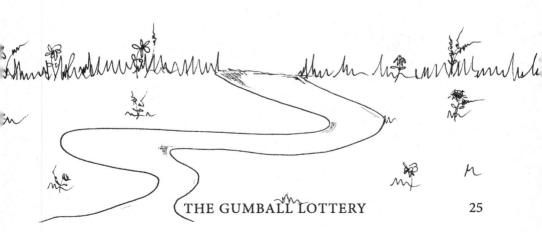

THE GUMBALL LOTTERY

CLOUD NINE
(& ALL THOSE OTHER CLOUDS, TOO)

Have you ever heard about Cloud Nine?
Happiness is at its highest there—
Where smiles can't be contained,
And you feel like you're floating on air.

But what about those other clouds?
I've heard they're pretty awesome, too.
Today I'll show what happens there;
I'll give a tour just for you.

SALLY DOLLAR

We'll start with cloud number Three
(Because it's fun to skip around).
That one's covered in trampolines!
We'll bounce backwards, forwards, up and down.

Next we'll visit number Six,
Where unicorns romp in the sun.
We'll pet them, feed them, brush their manes—
And even take a ride on one!

Then we'll hop to number Four.
It's covered with marshmallow cream!
We'll eat from the jellybean bushes there
And drink from the lemonade stream.

Number Two has an amusement park
With thrills as far as you can see!
There's no minimum height required—
And best of all, we'll ride for free!

THE GUMBALL LOTTERY   27

Then it's off to number Seven,
Where we'll swim in a GIGANTIC pool,
With a twisty slide that's a mile long
And a lazy river that's oh so cool!

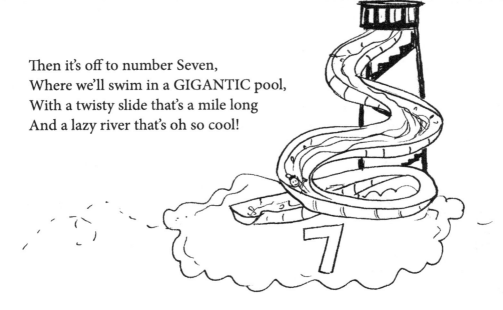

Number Five is filled with bubbles!
It'll be such a fun place to stop.
They come in all colors and shapes.
And guess what?! They never pop!

Next we'll head to number Eight,
Where mermaids splash and sing.
We'll listen as they tell fairy tales
And talk about magical things.

We'll save cloud One for the very last,
With the coziest bed you'll ever find.
Exhausted from our day's adventures,
We'll doze and dream about cloud Nine…

And all those other clouds, too.

WHERE IS PETE?!

Guess what?! It snowed today!
YIPPEE! WOO HOO! HIP HIP HOORAY!

And school was out—what a treat!
So, I went and found my best pal Pete.

Naturally, outside we went,
Making snowballs to our hearts' content.

Then we thought it'd be great fun
To make a really GIANT one.

So, we rolled the snow on the ground;
It grew and grew—so BIG and round!

We rolled it 'til it was the size of a KID!
It's hard to believe, but we really did!

I'm telling you, it was *so, so* neat—

Wait a minute…

Where is Pete?!

SALLY DOLLAR

FISHIN' FOR AN IDEA

There's an idea swimmin' in my head;

It's circlin' round and round.

I've got to somehow catch it,

So that I can write it down.

I've got to try and hook it,

Then reel it in some way.

Yep, I've made up my mind—

I'm goin' fishin' today.

LOST & FOUND

Somewhere in a town there is a school.
And in this school there is a place.
And in this place there is a box,
Full of items "just in case."

And on the box there is a sign,
Which is labeled "Lost & Found."
Inside the box are misplaced things,
In case their owners come around.

An umbrella left when the sun came out,
A book marked at chapter nine,
A harmonica which, when the show had ended,
Someone left behind.

A teddy bear with button eyes,
A pair of mismatched socks,
A silver ring with a shiny key—
Who knows what it unlocks?!

Some sunglasses without a lens,
One glove that's pink polka-dotted,
A lunch box with its contents removed
(Thankfully, before they rotted).

SALLY DOLLAR

A library card that has expired,
A mirror with a tiny dent,
A purple purse with fourteen cents—
Just waiting to be spent!

Every trinket has a story
Or a chapter left unread.
It's much more than a box of stuff—
It's a treasure trove instead!

ROLLER COASTER

Life is like a roller coaster,
With its ups and downs and looptie loos.

But we're on this thing together,
Through all the "OH NO!"s and all the "WOO HOO!"s.

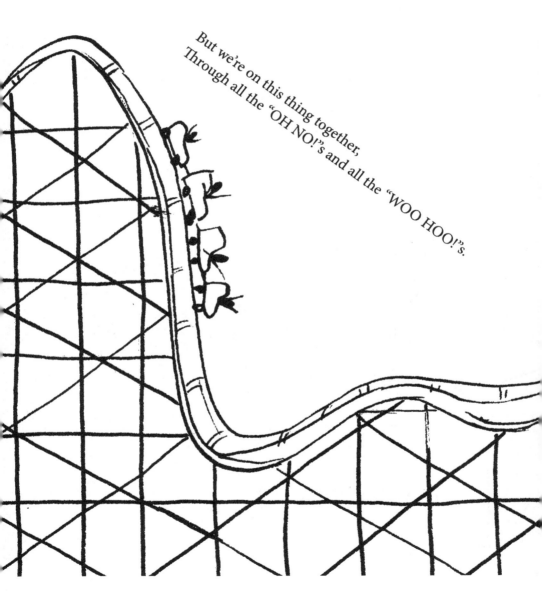

SALLY DOLLAR

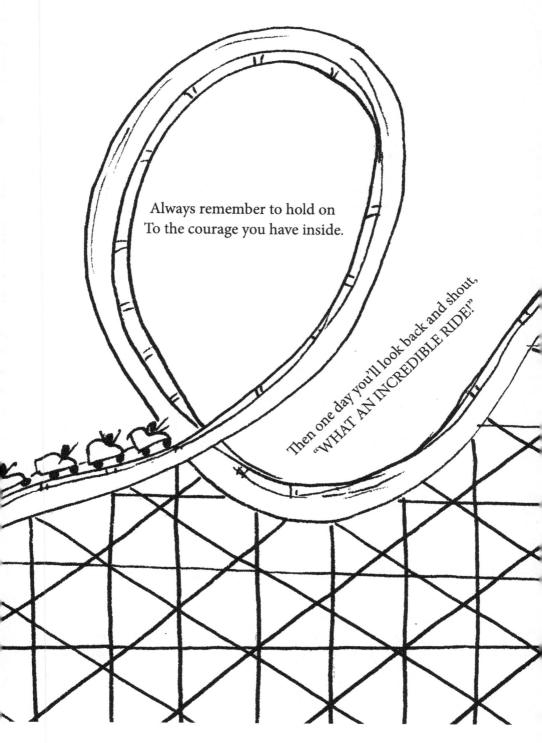

Always remember to hold on
To the courage you have inside.

Then one day you'll look back and shout,
"WHAT AN INCREDIBLE RIDE!"

THE GUMBALL LOTTERY

WHEN THE SUN GOES DOWN AT THE ZOO

When the sun goes down at the zoo
All of the animals shout, "WOO HOO!"
And every creature gathers 'round
To live it up and get down.

The monkeys sing; the elephants dance.
The giraffes limbo; the zebras prance.
The hyenas yell out with great glee.
It's the biggest party you'll ever see!

The hippos hula hoop; the apes, they giggle.
The chickens get funky; the llamas wiggle.
Inside their tanks, the fish do flips.
The parrots make punch, and everyone sips.

SALLY DOLLAR

The flamingos rock, and the **penguins roll.**
The peacocks strut, and the **tigers stroll.**
It's a fiesta full of wild fun
When the moon takes over for the sun.

Wombats, warthogs, beavers and bears,
Porcupines, pelicans, meerkats and mares—
All the beasts join right in,
And every night they do it again.

So if the question ever arose,
"Just what goes on when the zoo is *closed*?"
Now you know what the critters do
When the sun goes down at the zoo.

LITTLE LEROY

Leroy was a little boy
Who always tried his best.
And early on he realized
He was shorter than the rest.

But little Leroy had BIG dreams,
And he made up his mind
To never let his lack of height
Leave him far behind.

Leroy said, "I'll be a star!
I'll play basketball."
"No, no," some others said.
"You know you're much too small."

But little Leroy didn't care;
He knew he had the stuff.
For as much as he was small,
He was just as much tough.

When tryouts finally rolled around
And it was time to play,
He ignored the unkind comments,
And he went out anyway.

"But no," they said, "Leroy,
You're just not big enough."
But as much as some were tall,
He was just as much tough.

So he played and played with every bit
Of his great BIG might,
And not once was he discouraged
By his lack of height.

Working hard, he never let
His hopes fade or dim.
And now that Leroy's on the team,
They all look up to *him*.

SALLY DOLLAR

GET OUT!

Just beyond the walls of home
Is an awesome place to run and roam.
It stretches far, and it stretches wide—
A vast expanse that's called "outside."

Pry yourself from your device
And find some nature, where it's nice.
There are limitless things for you to do
Where the ceiling's endless and bright blue.

Take a hike down to the creek
Or start a round of hide-and-seek.
Play kickball with the kids next door.
If your games run out, make up some more!

Go feel the breeze upon your face.
Find some butterflies you can chase.
Count the clouds or climb a tree.
Best of all, this fun is free!

So, next time you are given the choice,
Go where you *don't* need your inside voice.
Put down that electronic contraption,
And go and get some outside action!

THE GUMBALL LOTTERY

41

JOURNEY OF THE REBEL SOCK

I'm tired of the same-old, same-old;
I'm weary of this routine.
I'd like to try something bold
After the washer's made me clean.

See, I'm a lone sock, and people say
That I'm odd (and a tiny bit strange).
But they can say whatever they may—
I'm just ready for a change.

Yesterday, while in the laundry,
I mapped out my escape.
But how will I get out of this quandary?
Well, my plans are taking shape.

First, I'll climb to the top of the hamper;
Then I'll hop off of its ledge.
Then across the floor I'll scamper,
Out the door to the water's edge.

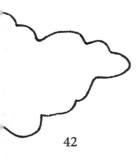

SALLY DOLLAR

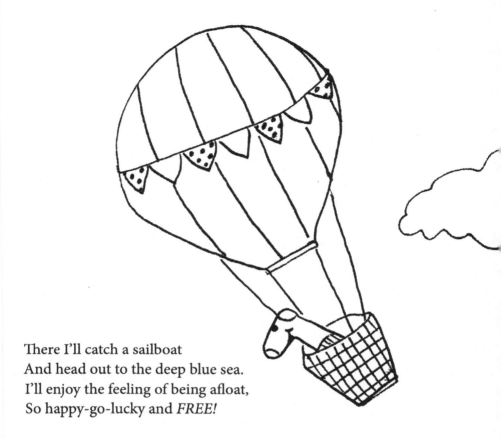

There I'll catch a sailboat
And head out to the deep blue sea.
I'll enjoy the feeling of being afloat,
So happy-go-lucky and *FREE!*

Next, I'll climb aboard a hot air balloon
And drift along in the sky.
I'll fly among clouds all afternoon,
Waving to birds as I pass by.

Then I'll hit the open road
On my shiny new motorbike.
I'll cruise through every zip code
All along the eastern turnpike!

When my journey's through at last,
I'll take a rest and I'll retire.
"Where *did* that sock go?!" others will ask,
While I snooze beneath the dryer.

UP OVER

Everyone knows that Australia
Is called the great "Down Under."
So, there must be an "Up Over," right?
And where is *that*, I wonder?

SALLY DOLLAR

EXERCISE YOUR NOGGIN

Physical health is great,
But I am here to witness—
It is utterly important
To give your brain some fitness.

"But how," you might ask,
"Do you work out your *brain*?"
Just like running a race,
You've got to work and plan and train.

The first step when warming up
Involves s t r e t c h i n g your mind.
Then your wheels will start to spin
On whatever task you find.

Read or play an instrument;
Write or do some math.
Search for new ideas, but…
Don't just take the easy path.

You'll only see results
When a challenge is involved.
Stick with it and practice—
You've got to have resolve!

We all know the positives
Of movin' and walkin' and joggin',
But it sure is beneficial
To exercise your noggin.

EIGHT WAYS TO MAKE A WISH

There's something that I really want;
I'd like to make a dream come true.
But to make my wish official,
There's some things I've gotta do.

First, I'll go out to my yard
And I'll find a four-leaf clover,
Then play wishbone tug-of-war
And claim victory when it's over.

I'll pretend that it's my birthday
And blow out candles on a cake,
Then toss a penny in the fountain
Beside the local lake.

SALLY DOLLAR

Next, I'll rub a genie's lamp
(I'll just buy one at the store.)
He'll grant me my BIG wish
(And if I'm lucky, I'll get two more!)

Then I'll find a dandelion
And blow its seeds into the wind,
While I rub my lucky rabbit's foot
To make my wish again.

Lastly, when my day is over
I'll gaze at the stars all night,
And find one that's falling down,
Being sure to time it *just* right.

Ok, that should take care of it!
I think that'll cover it, don't you?
What *exactly* is my wish?

Well, I can't tell…

'Cause then it won't come true.

THE GLASS

Some see a glass as half full.
"It's half empty," others may think.
I just wonder what's inside—
And if I should take a drink.

SALLY DOLLAR

MORE THAN PANCAKES

I love you more than pancakes and lemonade pies.

I love you more than s'mores and chili cheese fries.

I love you more than gummy bears and fizzy soda pop.

I love you more than anything—with a cherry on top.

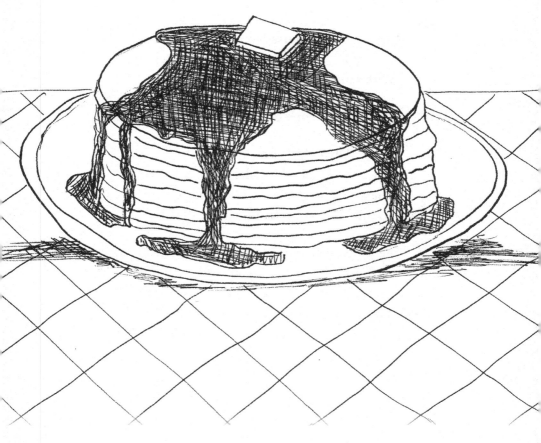

ON-UH-MOT-UH-PEE-UH

Let's talk about onomatopoeia…
(See above for how to pronounce it.)
It's when a word sounds like its noise—
Like a ball saying BOING! when you bounce it.

Let's think of more situations
When you would use words such as these.
Then you can use this concept yourself
With confidence, brains and great ease.

For example…

On a chilly day in winter
You let out a SHIVER, shake and say BRRR…
Then bury your head under your quilt,
While the cat cozies up with a PURR.

Then spring arrives (and so does pollen);
Your nose SNIFFS, and you yell ACHOO!
Meanwhile, the rooster welcomes the day
With a boisterous COCK-A-DOODLE-DOO!

SALLY DOLLAR

Summer rolls around—it's 4th of July!
Sounds of ZAP, BANG, KABOOM fill the night.
You watch as fireworks WHIZ through the sky,
While you CLAP and WOO HOO! with delight.

As autumn appears, the turkeys GOBBLE
While you sip on squash soup with a SLURP.
Satisfied with your yummy meal,
Your mouth lets out...a great...BIG...

"MMMMMMMMmmmmmmmmm"

Now, wait just a minute...

What did you *think* I would say at the end?
Always remember your manners, my friend!

PLAN B

I'm starting up a business;
I am selling lemonade.
But first I'll try it out myself,
And taste this product that I've made.

Hmm... Let's see...

I'm not sure about this first batch—
There's a lot of sour in my cup.
Think I'll add a bit more sugar,
So my customers will drink it up...

Ok, now it's way too sweet—
Talk about sugar overload!
I'll need to adjust my recipe
Before I sell this by the road.

Alrighty then, here goes...

Next batch, too bitter...

                Next batch, too bold...

Next batch, too warm...

                Next batch, too cold...

Next batch, too lemony...

                Next batch, too crummy...

Next batch, too watery...

                Next batch, too YUMMY...

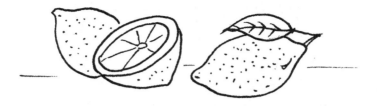

Uh-oh…

I've run out of lemonade!
Must be all this testing that I've done!

NOW WHAT?!

Well… I've got some lovely paper cups—
Would you like to purchase one?

THE GUMBALL LOTTERY   53

MY SEVEN SISTERS (AND ME)

In a little house on Sycamore Street
By the big, old sassafras tree,
Lives a family you should meet
With seven girls (and me).

First, there's Scarlet, tall and thin,
With a spirit gentle and true.
She loves to play her violin,
And her favorite color is blue.

The twins are next—they love to sing.
Their joy is uncontrolled.
Autumn enjoys the beauty of spring,
But Summer prefers the cold.

Ruby is a funny gal;
Her hair is full of curls.
She is a kind and loyal pal
And always wears her pearls.

SALLY DOLLAR

Then there's Daisy, who lies in the sun
While she dreams and dozes.
She takes her time and doesn't run—
She stops to smell the roses.

Virginia likes to dance and twirl;
She prances wherever she goes.
She wants to be a California girl
And tells everyone she knows.

Grace is the smallest one of all.
She loves to slide and swing.
She always totes around her doll,
And Grace is a clumsy little thing.

All of my sisters are the best;
They're exactly the family I need.

What's *my* name, you ask?

Well, they call me "Lucky,"
And, I'm a lucky brother indeed.

THE GUMBALL LOTTERY

MERMAID WISH

One night at the dinner table
Dad asked for fun (and just because),
"What'll you be when you grow up?"
And my sister's answer was…

"I want to be a mermaid!"
She squealed with a smile and great delight.
"Oh, to be a magic sea creature!
I've dreamed of it both day and night."

"In fact, I'd actually love it
If I became one very soon!"
So, at bedtime she made her wish
On a star to the left of the moon.

4 ft.

SALLY DOLLAR

Well, the next morning she woke up,
And what do ya know?! She got her wish!
She had the body of a girl—
And the tail of a fish.

To try out her new identity,
We went to the local pool.
She swam and splashed and dazzled—
Her aquatic tricks were just plain cool.

People came from miles around
To check out her mermaid show.
She twirled and dove and glided,
Backwards, forwards, high and low.

But her dream lasted only a day,
Then it was back to normal for Sis.
But she hangs on to the memory
Of the day she got her wish.

6 ft.

THE GUMBALL LOTTERY 57

THE SHEEP WHO COULDN'T SLEEP

There was a sheep who couldn't sleep,
So she tried with all her might
To fix her bedtime problem
When she laid down each night.

One evening she had an idea—
She knew exactly what to do.
"I'll try counting people!" she thought.
Then her sleep troubles were through.

SALLY DOLLAR

SLOW...DOWN

Slow...Down

No need to hurry, hurry, hurry.

Slow...Down

No need to worry, worry, worry.

Slow...Down

No need to go so fast, fast, fast.

Slow...Down

Make...those...little...moments...last.

WRANGLE UP A DREAM

It's time to begin an adventure;
It's time to try something new!
Let's take a chance and start right now.
I'll tell you what we should do…

Let's go capture a GIGANTIC dream!
It's not as hard as it may sound.
We should start looking right away—
Let's go chase one down!

First, gather up your confidence.
Next, make yourself a plan.
Then you're ready for the journey
(But don't forget where you began).

SALLY DOLLAR

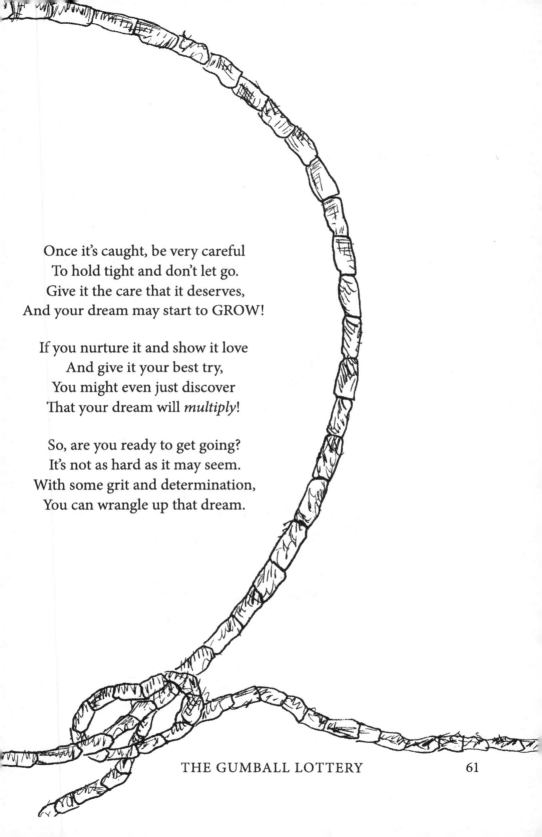

Once it's caught, be very careful
To hold tight and don't let go.
Give it the care that it deserves,
And your dream may start to GROW!

If you nurture it and show it love
And give it your best try,
You might even just discover
That your dream will *multiply*!

So, are you ready to get going?
It's not as hard as it may seem.
With some grit and determination,
You can wrangle up that dream.

THE GUMBALL LOTTERY

SALLY DOLLAR

RAINBOW SOUP

Here's a yummy recipe
You should give a try.
It's for a special feast
Made from rainbows in the sky.

Wait for a drizzly day
When the sun begins to shine,
Then follow these instructions
For a soup that's just divine!

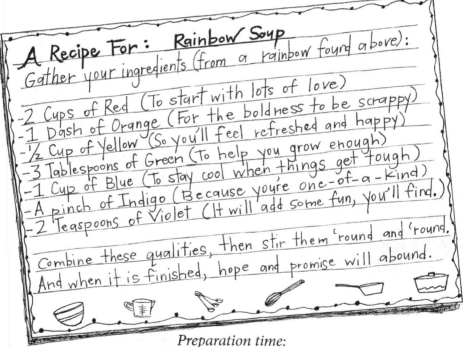

A Recipe For: Rainbow Soup
Gather your ingredients (from a rainbow found above):

-2 Cups of Red (To start with lots of love)
-1 Dash of Orange (For the boldness to be scrappy)
-½ Cup of Yellow (So you'll feel refreshed and happy)
-3 Tablespoons of Green (To help you grow enough)
-1 Cup of Blue (To stay cool when things get tough)
-A pinch of Indigo (Because you're one-of-a-kind)
-2 Teaspoons of Violet (It will add some fun, you'll find.)

Combine these qualities, then stir them 'round and 'round.
And when it is finished, hope and promise will abound.

Preparation time:
Depends on the weather.
Best served with friends gathered all together.

LITTLE THINGS

When BIG, fun things happen in your life
You may feel enthusiastic,
But *little* things are exciting, too,
And can really be fantastic.

Like when your hand digs in the pocket
Of a coat you wore last year
And fishes out a forgotten dollar,
So you say a little cheer.

Or when your **baby** sister chuckles
At something silly that you said,
Or you think you've goofed up on your test
But make an A on it instead.

When your mom bakes tasty brownies
And lets you lick the batter from the spoon,
Or you stay up past your bedtime
To point your telescope toward the moon.

SALLY DOLLAR

When you hear the tune of the ice cream truck
As it makes its way onto your street,
Or someone can recall your name
After the first time that you meet.

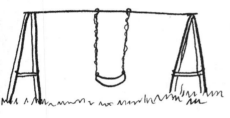

When your buddy kindly lets you take
The very last swing at the park,
Or when you see fireflies flicker
Their tiny lights when it gets dark.

When your teacher smiles and says, "Good job!"
After you gave it your best try,
Or when you look up with surprise
At a rainbow in the sky.

It's so much fun to find enjoyment
In things that seem so small,
Because sometimes *little* things
Are really BIG things after all.

THE CLIMB

You're at the edge of a mountain,
But do you take that climb?
Do you keep on moving forward
Or wait for a better time?

Do you decide to turn around,
Thinking you're not well prepared?
Do you feel a little nervous?
Do you feel a little scared?

Perhaps there *is* a reason
For this challenge that you face.
Maybe you were meant to be
Exactly in this place.

And maybe you've been given
A chance you shouldn't miss.
Perhaps you've been created
For such a time as this.

SALLY DOLLAR

ECHO!... ... ...ECHO!

HELLO!...HELLO!

IT'S SO NEAT...IT'S SO NEAT

TO HEAR MY VOICE.............................TO HEAR MY VOICE

REPEAT!..REPEAT!

I COULD DO THIS.....................................I COULD DO THIS

ALL DAY!...ALL DAY!

LET'S TRY IT!...LET'S TRY IT!

WHAT DO YOU SAY?................................I SAY LET'S DON'T!

MY PET POTATO

After much consideration
(And a little bit of thought),
I plan to adopt a potato
And name him Tater Tot.

This is the brightest idea
That I've come up with yet!
There are so many reasons
To make a potato my pet.

I'll never have to walk him;
He won't chew up the chair.
I won't need to bathe him
Or brush his scruffy hair.

SALLY DOLLAR

It will be so very easy
To teach him how to sit.
And if I leave him all alone,
He won't mind one bit.

All he'll really need
Is a spot upon my shelf.
It really is ingenious!
(If I do say so myself.)

Hmm…

This sounds a little boring,
So maybe on second thought,
I'll get a real live dog instead
And name *him* Tater Tot!

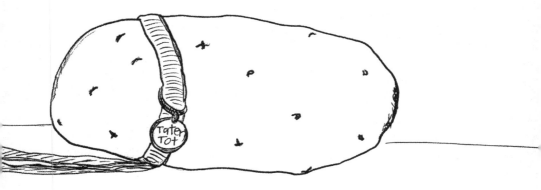

THE GUMBALL LOTTERY

BENNY & LENNY

There once was a boy named Benny
Who had a llama called Lenny.
They played games and had fun
In the hot summer sun
And had big adventures aplenty.

One day for something to do
They played fetch, which for Lenny was new.
So he kept running south
With the ball in his mouth,
Which left Benny alone feeling blue.

"I miss my dear friend!" the boy said,
Throwing a boomerang over his head.
Then back from the south,
Boomerang in his mouth,
Lenny ran home the same way that he fled.

CLOTHES FOR CHRISTMAS
(A HAIKU)

A package awaits…
Anticipation rises!
Socks. A Shirt. Bummer.

AN IDEA

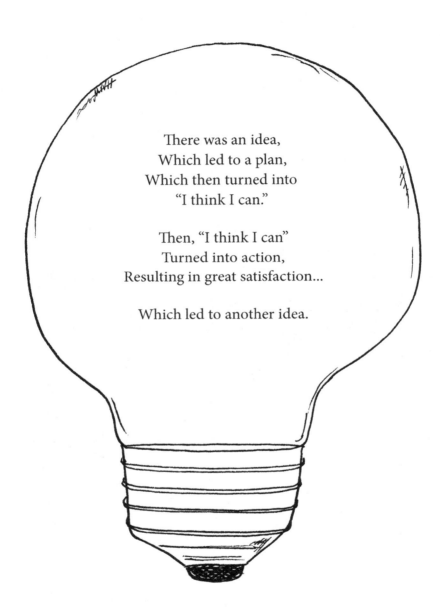

There was an idea,
Which led to a plan,
Which then turned into
"I think I can."

Then, "I think I can"
Turned into action,
Resulting in great satisfaction...

Which led to another idea.

SALLY DOLLAR

JUST A BOX

It's just a box, *right?*

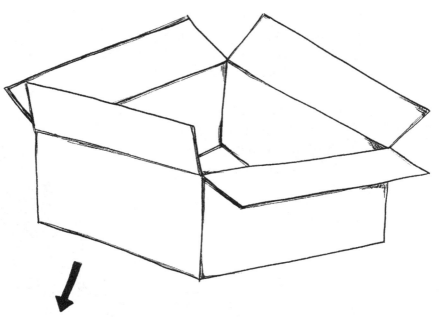

Or is it a playhouse?
A race car, a hat,
A castle, an airplane,
A bed for your cat?

A puppet theater,
A lemonade stand?
A little stage
For your troll doll band?

A sweet donut shop,
A fairy mansion?
A really awesome
Fort expansion?

A mailbox, a chair,
A time machine?
A movie night
Projection screen?

A pirate ship,
A cool space station?
Endless potential
For imagination?

Or is it just a box?

INVISIBLE INK

I've got an idea—it'll be so cool
To try out this plan I've got.
Let's have some fun with invisible ink.
Let's give it a go…Why not?!

See, I'll write the last word of each stanza
With my magical pen
And then you'll see if you can decode
Each message at the   .

SALLY DOLLAR

Here's how this little game will work—
First I'll compose the text.
Then you can try to figure out
Which word is written   .

Now, I know you could be thinking,
"What's the point? And why?"
Well, I really think it'd be quite swell
For me and you to   .

Well, have I convinced you yet?
What do you *really* think?
I just know it would be so fun
To write with invisible   !

SANTA IN SUMMER

When the holidays have ended,
It may seem like a bummer…
But not for Santa—
'Cause he *really* loves summer!

First, he makes his way south
To a warm destination,
Then he kicks off his boots
And takes a vacation.

76   **SALLY DOLLAR**

Instead of hot cocoa
He drinks lemonade,
While he chills and relaxes
And sits in the shade.

He rests and unwinds
With his toes in the sand,
And snorkels and scubas
And works on his tan.

He parasails and surfs
And snacks on shaved ice.
He hunts for seashells—
It's really quite nice!

He strolls on the beach
In comfy flip flops
And hosts festive luaus—
The fun never stops!

Until it's time to get back to work...

Oh well, there's always next summer.

ARTHUR DID IT!

My best pal is the greatest!
He's my imaginary friend.
And his name is Arthur—
We'll be buddies 'til the end!

Arthur and I are very close;
We're together all the time.
He always comes through for me
When I am in a bind.

For example, when Mom says,
"Your room's a big 'ol mess,"
I kindly reply with a smile,
"Arthur did it…I guess."

SALLY DOLLAR

And whenever Dad tells me,
"Time to clean. You know you should,"
I politely say with great respect,
"But Arthur said *he* would."

So next time when you're in a pinch,
I most highly recommend
You turn the blame right over
To your imaginary friend.

Wait just a minute…
Arthur has something to say—
He's telling me that it's not fair
To pick on him this way.

He says we should each do our part
To help clean up the mess.
He's so kind and honest…
I told you he's the BEST!

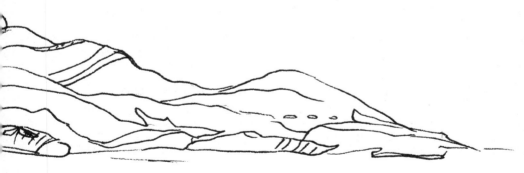

YES, NARWHALS ARE REAL!

Narwhals are often called
"Unicorns of the sea."
But sometimes people ask,
"Are they real? How can that be?!"

Well, actually they DO exist!
They are a type of whale.
They have bluish-grayish skin
And can look a little pale.

They live in Arctic waters
Where it's really, really cold.
They squeal and click and whistle—
It's how they talk, so I'm told...

And what about their horns?
What's the deal with those?
Well, it's actually a tooth
Just below their nose!

So, the next time someone asks,
You can answer with great zeal,
"Yes, indeed it is a fact—
Narwhals are REAL!"

SALLY DOLLAR

A...SLOTH...NAMED...BILL

There...once...was...a...sloth...named...Bill.
He...loved...to...relax...and...be...still.
Some said he was lazy,
Even calling him crazy.
But...Bill...replied..."Dudes...just...*CHILL*."

34 SCOOPS

Ooh, *listen!* I think I hear
The ice cream truck on our street.
Oh, wow, I'm so excited—
I can't wait to buy something sweet!

Ok, Mr. Ice Cream Man,
Let's see what I want to pick out…
So many choices; I can't decide.
They'll all taste good, no doubt.

Ok, I'll take one of *everything!*
I'll try a scoop of every flavor.
Pile them up on one cone—
What a treat for me to savor!

Chocolate and strawberry,
Rocky road, banana delight,
Butter pecan, birthday cake—
This'll be out of sight!

SALLY DOLLAR

Pistachio, blue raspberry,
Bubble gum, cotton candy,
Peanut butter and vanilla—
Man, oh man, what a dandy!

Lemon supreme, caramel crunch,
Passion fruit, key lime pie…
So many varieties—
This cone's gonna reach the sky!

Coconut, orange, mint chocolate chip,
Tutti frutti, cookies and cream,
Maple walnut, pumpkin spice—
What a delicious dream!

Cookie dough, cherry ripple,
English toffee, pineapple ice,
Honey almond, mango, peach—
This'll taste so, so nice!

Hazelnut, peppermint…
The list goes on forever!
Neapolitan, butterscotch—
This is the Best. Day. Ever.

And of course, it's pretty obvious—
I want a cherry and sprinkles on top.
It will be so very yummy…
This cone will NEVER STOP!

Now, how in the world am I gonna eat this THING?!

THE GUMBALL LOTTERY   83

A DONUT

A friend once asked the question,
"If you were a food, what would you be?"
And I replied, "A donut,"
'Cause they're sweet and well-rounded like me.

(Plus, I really like donuts.)

84   SALLY DOLLAR

AND SO THE STORY GOES...

How does a story begin?

Well, it starts with a letter, then a word,
Becoming part of a sentence you write.
Then those sentences form a chapter,
Bringing your story to light.

And once it's finished, it's read and told,
And borrowed and shared, until it takes hold.

Eventually, its impact grows—
And so the story goes...

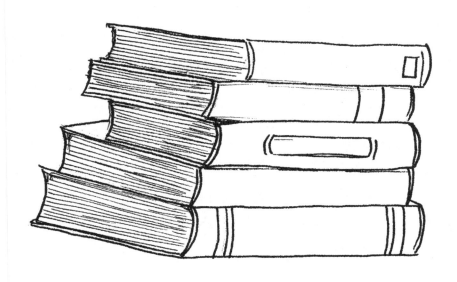

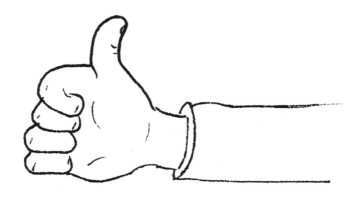

BE A DOER

Be a DOER.

Don't be a procrastinator,
Telling yourself, "I'll do it later."

Don't be a "not today"-er
Or an "I can't do it" sayer.

Be a thinker and a planner;
Be a "Yes, indeed I *can*"-er.

Be an explorer and a goer;
Be a "Yes, indeed I *know*"-er.

Be a creator; Be a schemer,
A world-changer and a dreamer.

Be a mover and a shaker,
A bold barrier breaker,
An innovation maker,
A confident risk taker.

Whatever you do…Be a DOER.

SALLY DOLLAR

SMILE

When you're getting ready for the day
And wondering what to wear,
Be sure to put on a smile—
It's an accessory you can share!

(And best of all, it's FREE.)

THE THING ABOUT KUDZU

The thing about kudzu is…

It grows

& grows

& grows

& grows

& grows

& grows

& grows

& grows!

And when will it stop?
Well, no one really knows!

SALLY DOLLAR

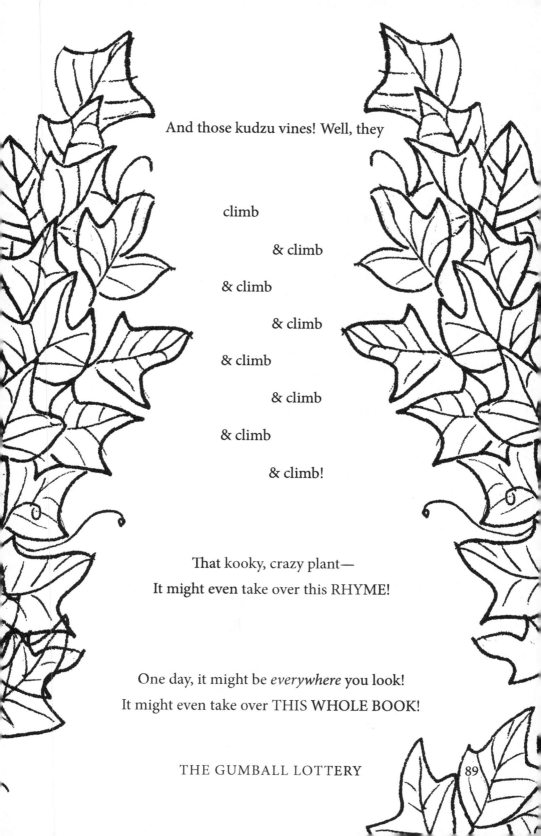

And those kudzu vines! Well, they

climb

    & climb

& climb

    & climb

& climb

    & climb

& climb

    & climb!

That kooky, crazy plant—
It **might even** take over this RHYME!

One day, it might be *everywhere* you look!
It might even take over THIS **WHOLE BOOK!**

THE GUMBALL LOTTERY

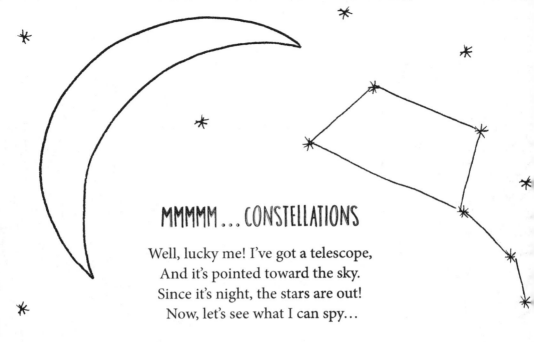

MMMMM...CONSTELLATIONS

Well, lucky me! I've got a telescope,
And it's pointed toward the sky.
Since it's night, the stars are out!
Now, let's see what I can spy...

Oooh! I found the Big Dipper!
And I see the little one, too.
Okay, yep, that's Ursa Minor—
You can't beat this nighttime view!

Wait, I see a few others
I haven't learned about in school...
Man, oh man, what I'm looking at
Is really, really cool!

That one looks like a milkshake!
And there's some giant fries!
And there's a great big burger
Right before my very eyes!

I spy a slice of pizza;
Oh goody, that's my fave!
And there's a plate of nachos—
It's really those I crave.

SALLY DOLLAR

Wow! Is that a piece of *bacon*?
Is that what I'm looking at?!
And over there, some brussels sprouts—
Bet my parents would like that…

All of this awesome stargazing
Has put me in such a great mood.
Plus, it's made me realize
I'm kind of hungry for some food…

How about some pizza and nachos?
(Let's skip the brussels sprouts.)

REFRIGERATOR GALLERY

In our kitchen (right by the stove)
There's a magnificent display…
Our fridge is covered in art!
And it's amazing, I would say.

There's a cotton ball snowman,
A macaroni noodle cat,
A finger print rainbow,
And a stick man with a hat.

There's a paper plate fish
With glitter on its fins,
And a photo booth picture
Of me and my best friends.

There's a pom-pom monster
With three googly eyes,
And a third place ribbon
That I once won as a prize.

And colorful alphabet magnets
Hold the masterpieces in place.
So much art to peruse and ponder…
It's such a creative space!

SALLY DOLLAR

And my mom, well she's the curator—
She's got a great eye for that stuff.
She's quite the avid collector
And can never get enough!

All of those famous museums
Just really can't compare...
It's the most impressive gallery
You'll find anywhere!

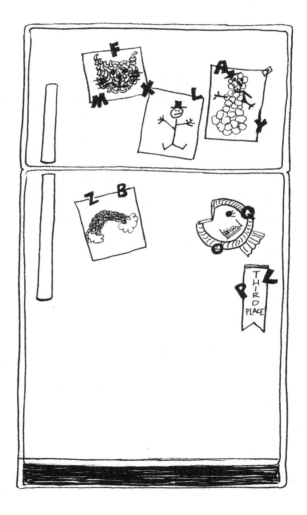

NOT
THIS IS ^ THE END

Have you ever heard the saying,
"All good things must come to an end?"
Well, this is only the beginning.
This is not the end, my friend.

If you reach your story's finish,
There's another for you to enjoy.
So, go look for your next adventure.
This is not the end, my boy.

There are plenty of doors you'll find
In this colossal world.
Just search for one to open.
This is not the end, my girl.

I hope you'll always remember
Until we meet again—
It is only the beginning;
This is clearly *not* the end.

SALLY DOLLAR

ABOUT THE AUTHOR

A graduate of the University of Tennessee and the University of Alabama at Birmingham, Sally has worked in the communications and education fields. She lives in Birmingham with her husband Chris, three kiddos and two fish, all of whom enthusiastically served as the focus group for this book. (Although the fish didn't provide much feedback, they did listen intently during manuscript readings.)

Sally grew up with a love of words and an appreciation for the magic that they hold (thanks, in part, to her word-loving, English-teaching mother). From reciting poetry at her kindergarten talent show to working at the local newspaper as a teenager, she found her THING at an early age—crafting words into sentences and sentences into stories. And some of those stories just happen to rhyme. Eventually, Sally decided to take a chance with *The Gumball Lottery*—and she's so glad she did.

SALLY DOLLAR

ABOUT THE ILLUSTRATOR

Growing up in the Mississippi Delta (where the arts continue to flourish), Rorie discovered her THING as an imaginative five year-old. She could often be found escaping with her sister to their backyard playhouse to draw, write and create.

A graduate of Samford University, she currently works as a pediatric occupational therapist. This calling allows her to incorporate her love of art into helping elementary school students with fine motor activities. She has been a featured artist for Southern Living at Home, illustrating and painting everything from landscapes to pet portraits. She continues to nurture this passion as opportunities come her way—and especially enjoys teaching art to children. Residing in Birmingham with her husband Chad and two kiddos, Rorie still happily considers art as her escape (just like all those years ago in that playhouse).

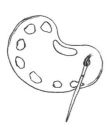  

Made in the USA
Coppell, TX
02 December 2019

12234742R00066